P9-CQZ-496

3 2148 00064 9862

Discard

JE
BUT

Butler, Stephen

The Mouse and the
apple

$14.93   Discard

DATE DUE

MIDDLETOWN PUBLIC LIBRARY
700 WEST MAIN RD
MIDDLETOWN RI 02840

05/20/1994

6/94

BAKER & TAYLOR BOOKS

To Rebecca, Joanne, Cheryl, Charlotte, Charlene,
Danielle, and Ross with love

The Mouse and the Apple copyright © 1994 by Frances Lincoln Limited.

Copyright © 1994 by Stephen Butler

First published in Great Britain by Frances Lincoln Limited,

4 Torriano Mews, London NW5 2R2, England.

All rights reserved. No part of this book may be reproduced or utilized in any form or by any
means, electronic or mechanical, including photocopying, recording, or by any information storage
or retrieval system, without permission in writing from the Publisher. Inquiries should be
addressed to Tambourine Books, a division of William Morrow & Company, Inc.,

1350 Avenue of the Americas, New York, New York 10019.

Printed in Hong Kong

Library of Congress Cataloging in Publication Data

Butler, Stephen. The Mouse and the apple/by Stephen Butler.—1st ed. p. cm.

Summary: Other animals come and go while Mouse waits patiently for a ripe apple to fall from
a tree. [1. Mice—Fiction. 2. Animals—Fiction. 3. Patience—Fiction.] I. Title. PZ7.B9776Mo 1994

[E]—dc20 93-15951 CIP AC ISBN 0-688-12810-6 (trade).—ISBN 0-688-12811-4 (lib.)

1 3 5 7 9 10 8 6 4 2

First U.S. edition

MIDDLETOWN PUBLIC LIBRARY
JE
BUT

The MOUSE and the Apple

by Stephen Butler

TAMBOURINE BOOKS  NEW YORK

June 22, 1994

One day Mouse saw a lovely ripe apple in a tree.
It was red and shiny, and it looked delicious.
Mouse waited for the apple to fall.

Along came Hen.
"Hello, Mouse! What are you doing?"
"I'm waiting for the apple to fall," said Mouse.
"That's a good idea," said Hen hopefully.
"I'll wait with you."

So Mouse and Hen waited for the apple to fall.

Along came Goose.
"Hello, Mouse! Hello, Hen! What are you doing?"
"We're waiting for the apple to fall," said Hen.
"Apples are my favorite," said Goose greedily.
"I'll wait with you."

So Mouse, Hen, and Goose waited for the apple to fall.

Along came Goat.
"Hello, Mouse! Hello, Hen! Hello, Goose!
What are you doing?"
"We're waiting for the apple to fall," said Goose.
"I love apples," said Goat hungrily. "I'll wait with you."

So Mouse, Hen, Goose, and Goat waited for the apple to fall.

Along came Cow.
"Hello, Mouse! Hello, Hen! Hello, Goose!
Hello, Goat! What are you doing?"
"We're waiting for the apple to fall," said Goat.
"I was just thinking about apples," said Cow, licking her lips.
"I'll wait with you."

So, Mouse, Hen, Goose, Goat, and Cow all waited for the apple to fall.

They waited.
And they waited.
And they waited.

Mouse waited patiently, but Cow, Goat, Goose, and Hen soon grew restless. They thought up ways to make the apple fall.

"I'll fly up and knock it down," said Hen, and
she ran toward the tree, flapping her wings.

But she tripped and fell on her beak with a bump.

"I'll honk it down," said Goose.
He opened his beak wide. "Hook! Honk! Honk!"

But the apple didn't move.

"I'll butt it down," said Goat.
He ran at the tree and butted it as hard as he could.

But the apple didn't budge.

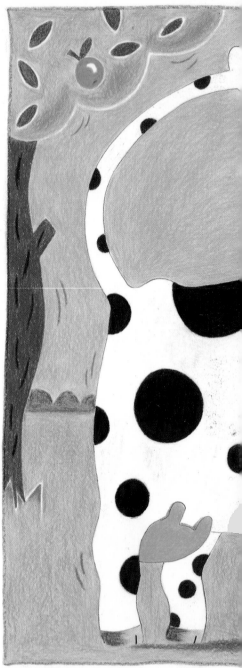

"I've got a good idea!" cried Cow.
She jumped up and down on all four hooves.

The tree trembled and the apple began to quiver.

"Everybody jump!" cried Cow, jumping up and down.
Goat jumped up and down.
Goose jumped up and down.
Hen jumped up and down.

The tree shook and the apple wobbled,
but still the apple didn't fall.
Meanwhile, Mouse waited patiently.

"Let's go," Cow said grumpily.
"That apple's probably rotten anyway."
"Or sour," said Goat.
"Or hard," said Goose.
"Or soft," said Hen.

Now only Mouse was left.
All of a sudden the shiny red apple
fell to the ground with a plop!

It wasn't rotten or sour or hard or soft.
It was the crunchiest, sweetest, most delicious
apple Mouse had ever tasted!